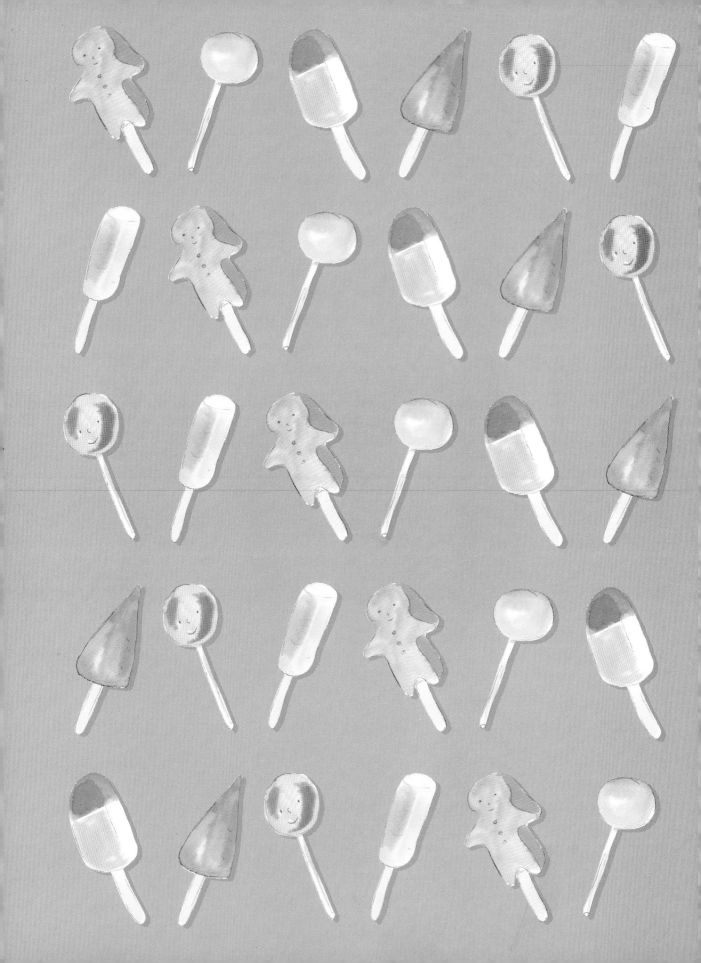

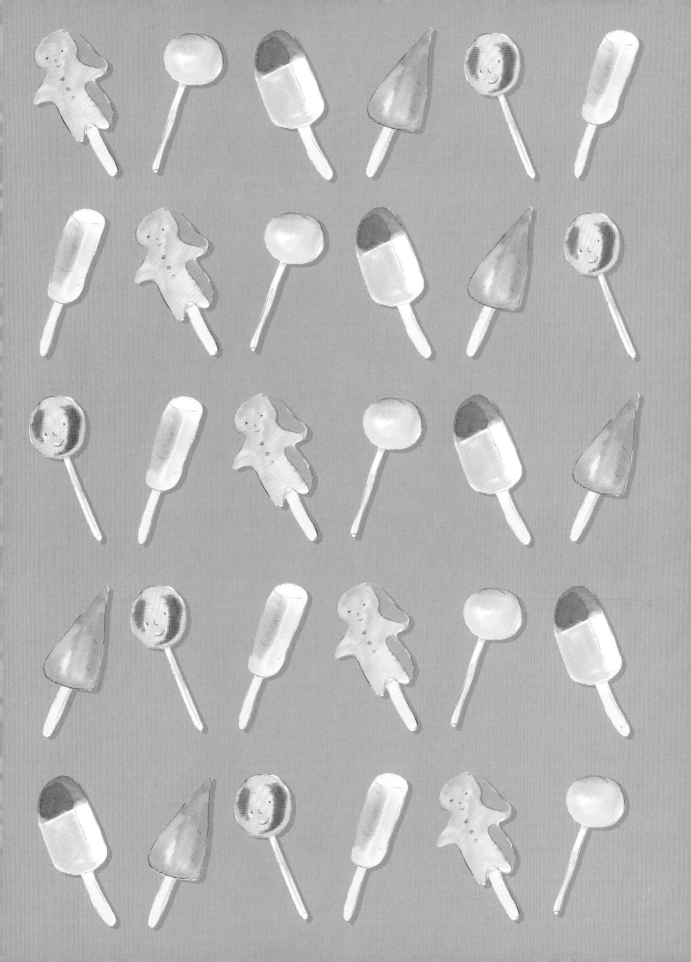

Lollipops

Doctor Proctor

and other rhymes

Original poems by **John Foster**
Illustrated by **John Wallace**

Oxford University Press

Oxford University Press, Great Clarendon Street, Oxford OX2 6DP

Oxford New York
Athens Auckland Bangkok Bogota Bombay
Buenos Aires Calcutta Cape Town Dar es Salaam Delhi
Florence Hong Kong Istanbul Karachi
Kuala Lumpur Madras Madrid Melbourne
Mexico City Nairobi Paris Singapore
Taipei Tokyo Toronto Warsaw

and associated companies in
Berlin Ibadan

Oxford is a trade mark of Oxford University Press

Text copyright © John Foster 1998
Illustrations copyright © John Wallace 1998
First published 1998

A CIP catalogue record for this book is available
from the British Library

ISBN 0 19 276180 3

Printed in Belgium

Contents

Doctor Proctor

Doctor Proctor hired a helicopter
And flew to Timbuctu.
When he telephoned the Queen,
She asked him where he'd been,
And he said, 'I haven't a clue.'

Jason Mason

Jason Mason jumped in a basin
To give himself a wash.
He got a big surprise
'Cause he didn't realize
It was full of orange squash.

Marty Smarty

Marty Smarty went to a party
In her jumbo jet.
After tea
She jumped in the sea
And got her pants all wet.

The skipping show

Skip one. Skip two.
Skip to my Lucy. Skip to my Lou.

Skip one. Skip—two, three.
Skip for you and skip for me.

Skip one, two—three, four, five.
Skip to my jump. Skip to my jive.

Skip one, two, three. Skip four, five, six.
Skip to my pick. Skip to my mix.

Skip one, two, three, four, five, six, seven.
Skip down to earth. Skip up to heaven.

Skip seven, eight—nine, ten.
Skip to my Basil. Skip to my Ben.

Skip up. Skip down.
Skip high. Skip low.
Skip with a smile
In the skipping show.

Feet

Feet are for kicking up leaves and snow.
Feet are for marching to and fro.
Feet are for running up and downhill.
Feet are for standing straight and still.
Feet are for hopping, feet are for skipping.
Feet are for sliding and sometimes slipping!
Feet are for splashing in puddles and rain.
Feet are for jumping again and again.
Feet are for stamping when you're mad.
Feet are for dancing when you're glad.

Shoes

Red shoes, blue shoes,
Old shoes, new shoes.

Shoes that are comfy,
Shoes that are tight,
Shoes that are black,
Shoes that are white.

Shoes with buckles,
Shoes with bows,
Shoes that are narrow
And pinch your toes.

Shoes that are yellow,
Shoes that are green,
Shoes that are dirty,
Shoes that are clean.

Shoes for when it's cold,
Shoes for when it's hot.
Shoes with laces
That get tangled in a knot!

Paint

Paint on your clothes.
Paint on your skin.
Paint on your nose.
Paint on your chin.

Paint on your elbows.
Paint on your thumb.
Paint on your knees.
Paint on your tum.

Paint on your cheeks.
Paint on your hair.
Paint on your ankles.
How did it get there?

Paint on your shirt.
Paint on your dress.
Paint all over you.
Oh, what a mess!

Roly poly plasticine

Roly poly plasticine.
What can you make?
A big fat sausage.
A flat pancake.

Roly poly plasticine.
Roll a round ring.
A necklace for a princess.
A crown for a king.

Roly poly plasticine.
What can you make?
A bendy banana.
A long thin snake.

Swing me

Swing me, swing me, swing me high.
Swing me so that I can fly.

Higher, higher, higher, please
Till I'm up above the trees.

Swing me, swing me, swing me high.
Swing me till I touch the sky.

Going for a swim

On hot summer days, at the end of school,
We go for a swim in the swimming pool.

As soon as I'm ready, I jump straight in.
I gasp as cold water splashes my skin.

I paddle across and cling to the side,
Then pull myself out to go on the slide.

I check that it's safe, then let myself go,
With a splash I crash in the water below.

I go under water, but I don't care.
I come to the surface and breathe in some air.

Then I swim as fast as I can to the side
And I climb back up for another slide!

Rainy day sounds

On rainy days
the rain slaps and taps
against window panes.

On rainy days
the rain drops and plops
into puddles in lanes.

On rainy days
the rain giggles and gurgles
as it slurps down drains.

Ten tall sunflowers

Ten tall sunflowers
Standing by the trees.
Ten tall sunflowers
Blowing in the breeze.
Ten bedraggled sunflowers
Dripping in the rain.
Ten smiling sunflowers
When the sun comes out again.

Where are you going, Jenny?

Where are you going, Jenny,
Dressed in green?

I'm going to the palace
To dine with the Queen.

Where are you going, Jenny,
Dressed in red?

I'm going for a ride
On Santa's sled.

Where are you going, Jenny,
Dressed in blue?

I'm going to have tea
With a kangaroo.

Where are you going, Jenny,
Dressed in white?

I'm going for a sail
On the ship of the night.

Shampoo Sally

Shampoo Sally
Washing her hair,
Splashing soapsuds everywhere.

Soapsuds in the water.
Soapsuds in the air.
Soapsuds here and soapsuds there.

Shampoo Sally
Rinsing her hair,
Splashing water everywhere.

Water on the bath mat.
Water on the floor.
Water dripping down the bathroom door.

Shampoo Sally
Washing her hair,
Soapsuds and water everywhere.
Shampoo Sally doesn't care.

Hairy scary spider

Hairy scary spider
On the bathroom wall.
Hairy scary spider
Don't you dare fall!

Hairy scary spider
Hanging by a thread,
What if you should fall
And land on my head!

Hairy scary spider
Find somewhere else to play.
Hairy scary spider
Please go away!

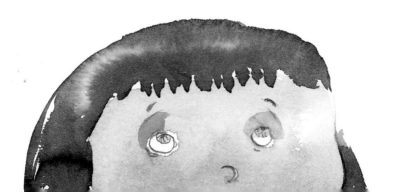

Walking round the zoo

Walking round the zoo,
What did I see?

A prowling tiger
That growled at me.

Walking round the zoo,
What did I see?

A parrot that squawked
And winked at me.

Walking round the zoo,
What did I see?

An elephant that waved
Its trunk at me.

Walking round the zoo,
What did I see?

A monkey that pointed
And laughed at me!

The snowman says

I like it when it's cold,
When the north wind blows,
When it snows and it freezes
My nose and my toes.

I don't like it when it's hot,
When it's sunny all day,
When my nose is runny
And I melt away.

It's snowed

It's snowed! It's snowed!
It's blocked the road.
The school is closed today!
Come on! Come on!
Get your wellies on!
We're going out to play.

We'll get the sledge
Out of the shed
And go up by the mill.
We'll sit upright
And cling on tight
As we hurtle down the hill.

We'll roll about.
We'll laugh and shout,
And make snowballs to throw.
Come on! Come on!
Get your anorak on!
Come out and play in the snow.

SCHOOL
CLOSED

Leap like a leopard

Leap like a leopard.
Dive like a whale.
Creep like a caterpillar.
Crawl like a snail.

Scuttle like a spider.
Slither like a snake.
Slide like a duck
On a frozen lake.

Skip like a lamb.
Jump like a frog.
Stalk like a cat.
Scamper like a dog.

Plod like an elephant.
Prowl like a bear.
Shuffle like a tortoise.
Sprint like a hare.

Strut like a peacock
With feathers held high.
Glide like an eagle—
The lord of the sky.

My special friend

At night when it's dark
I like to pretend
That my bed is guarded
By my special friend.

I like to pretend
As I snuggle down tight
That my friend will guard me
As I sleep through the night.

Why?

Why do the hands
On the clock on the wall
Always seem to
Crawl, crawl, crawl,
When you're sitting around
With nothing to do
But twiddle your thumbs
And tap your shoe?

Why do the hands
On the clock seem to fly
And time to go racing
By, by, by,
When you're having fun,
Then you hear Mum say,
'It's time to pack
Your toys away'?

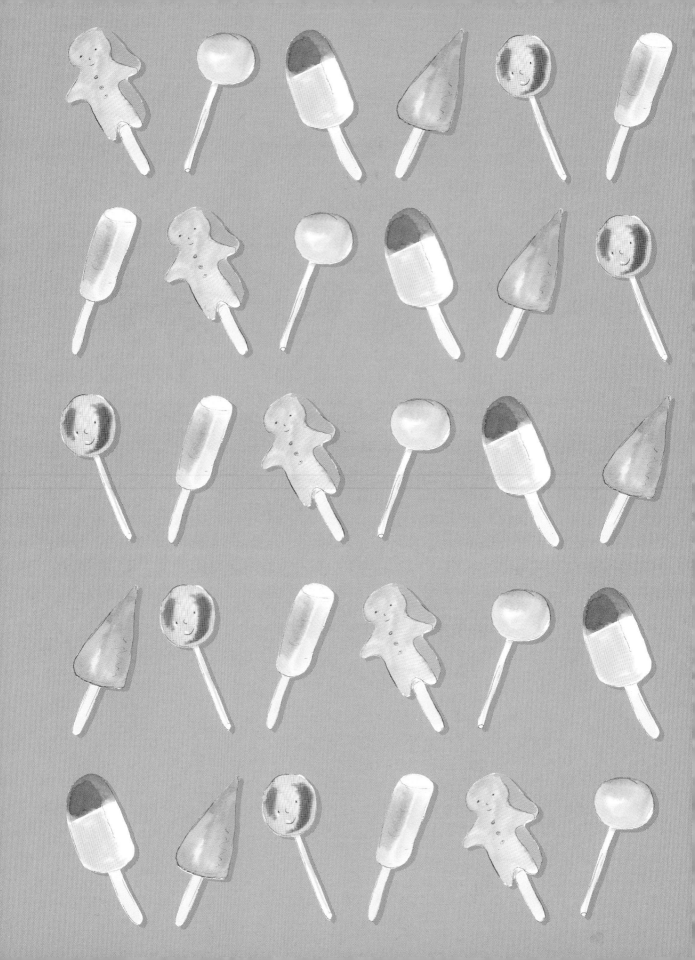

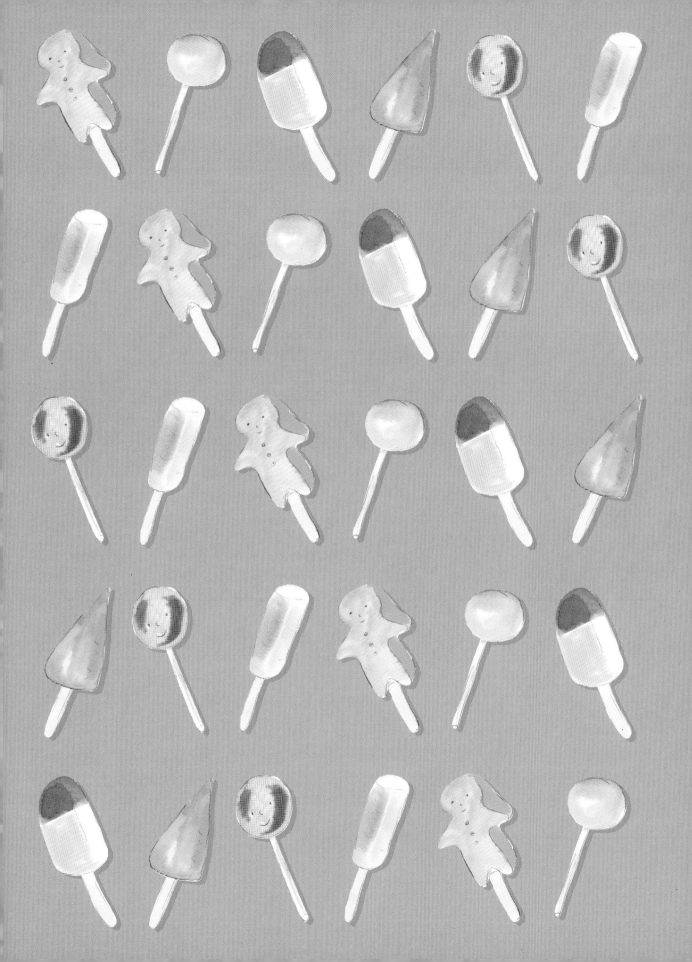